AF416508

HE SAID ALWAYS... HE LIED!

Deception: He Lied Miniseries

Book 2

Daphne Dennis

TLM Publishing House

Copyright

Copyright © 2022 Daphne Dennis, TLM Publishing House

All rights reserved. No portion of this book may be reproduced in any form without permission from the publisher, except as permitted by U.S. copyright law. For permissions contact: info@tlmpublishinghouse.com

Social Stamina – 1,2,3 Let's Go!

Titles to help look at things from other perspectives and strengthen your mindset.

The Great Ascension–1,2,3 Let's Go!

Titles to help you gain focus and climb the ladder of success!

How to Start – 1,2,3 Let's Go!

Titles to help you with step-by-step, must-have knowledge of the business world and personal experiences.

Top 10 Questions to Ask Before You…1,2,3 Let's Go!

Titles with must-have questions (and logic behind) for many of life's daily and major decisions.

Find our fiction below!

https://www.ttpublishinghouse.com/legendsreborn

https://www.ttpublishinghouse.com/7wishes

https://www.ttpublishinghouse.com/mallcadet

Social Media

Facebook: tlmpublishinghouse

Website: www.TTpublishinghouse.com

Want to Read for Free?

You may qualify for a spot on our Advance Reader Copy group.

Never heard of an ARC Group?

Simply put, it's a small group of people who are interested in a specific genre and are invited to read books before they're published.

Your feedback can help alter the storyline or even catch an elusive typo!

You're asked to provide an honest review when it is published, and that's it!

You read for free!

Go now to confirm your interest in the ARC Group!
https://www.ttpublishinghouse.com/joinTLMarc

Contents

Memorial 1

Herman 8

Ice Cream 21

Let's Visit.. 30

Memorial

Debbie stared absentmindedly at the painting on the lavender wall of her kitchen. It was The Starry Night by Vincent Van Gogh. *I wonder where that is. I wonder if I could go there.* She would rather be anywhere other than where she was.

She glanced at the other pictures on her wall, mostly family portraits, before sorting through her pile of mail. Most of the envelopes were bills, which she looked at begrudgingly before tossing them on the coffee table with a huff. Her Maltipoo, Fluffy, ran over to her, wagging his tail.

"Do you want to sort through this mail?" she asked him. "It would be incredibly helpful to me." Fluffy barked. He seemed to be keen.

"I know that you would if you could. Sometimes you're the only one who understands me."

She was behind in going through her mail. The task was cast aside during recent events. Her husband, Ed, had recently moved out. She suspected he was having an affair.

She had given him an ultimatum to tell her what was happening or to leave. Her heart shattered when he agreed to leave and went to pack his bags.

Then she noticed a slightly different-looking envelope. A single, beige-colored unopened letter lay amidst many white opened ones. *Hmm, what's this?* She picked it up and opened it. It was a letter from Judy's family inviting Debbie to a memorial service.

The memorial service is today. Debbie would never forget when she found Judy's body on the bedroom floor of the cabin. Judy's death still felt surreal. It would forever be seared in Debbie's brain when she found Judy lying on the cabin floor, dead.

Debbie couldn't pretend that it didn't unnerve her. Judy was someone she had known personally and considered a friend. Knowing that she was murdered made it hard for Debbie to sleep at night. *It would be ill-mannered if I didn't attend her funeral, wouldn't it? I really don't want to go.*

She ascended the stairs to her bedroom, the décor she had created herself. *Lotta freakin' good that did. Now I am here by myself. Why did I put so much effort into designing this room?*

She put on a black short-sleeved turtleneck paired with a long straight 8-panel skirt of the same color that reached just below her knees. *Ugh, black. I look terrible in black.*

The dark color was a stark contrast to her light skin. Debbie debated on whether she should wear flats or heels. *Knowing my recent luck, I'll probably fall and break my neck.* She opted for wearing her flats. *No need for a double funeral over a pair of cute heels.*

Deciding that she was dressed appropriately enough to pay her respects, she went downstairs, locked the door, and left. She ensured that the doors were properly locked and the windows shut tight. *The killer is still out there somewhere. I can't be too careful. It's better to be safe than sorry.*

The evergreen trees surrounding her driveway provided year-round seclusion and much-needed greenery during the winter months. She carefully dropped herself into the seat of her red sedan, her hands clenched on the steering wheel. *I still can't believe Judy was murdered.*

He Said Always... He Lied!

Judy's daughter's home, where the funeral was being conducted, was only a 10-minute drive away. As she drove, she passed many trees and vineyards, which were especially lovely when the sunlight poked through the trees like it was doing that day. She arrived quickly and parked her car on the street.

Debbie knocked on the door. Judy's daughter was a pretty woman in her 30s. "We're all in the living room," she said. Debbie walked into the living room.

She noticed fewer people at this memorial service than expected; she knew Judy had many friends. And, if that wasn't baffling enough, Dan, Judy's husband, wasn't there at all. *No one seemed to be talking about the fact that Dan had completely disappeared off the face of the earth. The man isn't even attending his own wife's memorial service? What the hell is going on, and why am I the only one who seems to notice how odd this is?*

Debbie looked around and casually walked toward Judy's daughter, who was busy talking with the family's close friends. "Hi. Sorry for interrupting, but can I talk to you for a minute?" Debbie asked.

Judy's daughter looked at her for a second before excusing herself from the conversation. She then ushered Debbie into the kitchen. "What do you want to talk about?" Judy's daughter asked, leaning back on the marbled kitchen island while she crossed her arms.

She looked fine aside from the bags under her eyes and sunken cheeks; her eyes weren't moist or puffy, unlike what Debbie would have expected. Again, *odd.*

"Your name has slipped my mind," Debbie said, embarrassed.

"It's Sandra," the woman replied. *That's right. I remember that now. Little Sandy with pigtails.* The last time Debbie had seen the girl, she had only been 10 years old.

"I'm so sorry about your mother. It's just that I noticed your father isn't here... By the way, where is Dan? Is he coming? I haven't seen him in a long time. Is he alright? How is he holding up? " Debbie asked, with genuine concern in her voice.

"Sadly, my mom and dad separated a while ago," she started, shifting her weight onto her other foot. "He's living in the city now." Judy's daughter shook her head with a frown, her eyes closed as she took a deep, painful breath. "We don't talk to him anymore. We're all too mad that he just left without a word. If only he hadn't left mom, then perhaps mom would still be alive..."

Debbie pursed her lips in sympathy, walking closer to comfort the young woman with a pat on her shoulder. "I'm sorry to hear about that. And I'm sorry to hear about your mom. She was a lovely and kind woman."

"Yes." Her daughter choked on the word, thanking Debbie with a nod and a smile. "Yes, she was."

They returned to the living room. Hushed whispers and murmurs of condolences were said left and right. An eerie silence settled in the room once the whispers and murmurs ceased.

The guests were a mix of old, young, and middle-aged individuals, all wearing black. Strangely, it seemed like no one wanted to be there. They looked at their watches and cell phones to check the time. It seemed like no one was crying; even Judy's family members had dry eyes.

None of the guests shed a tear except one. The elderly man's face was marked with blemishes, age spots, and etched with wrinkles. White hair sat atop his head. His eyes appeared to be wide open all the time. She could see the whites of his eyes around the entire perimeter of the iris. She knew exactly who he was. He was Judy's boss at the nuclear lab: Herman Miller.

***

He Said Always... He Lied!

Debbie yawned. It was getting late. Fatigue was finally hitting her as her eyelids got heavier. She was supposed to be getting ready for bed, but instead, she was reminiscing in her bedroom.

She didn't understand why Ed had been acting so mysterious, why he was never home. That part was bizarre because he was newly retired from being a nuclear physicist at the lab. Of course, Debbie knew something was up because there was so much money from their bank account that he had withdrawn, and he refused to tell her anything about it. In fact, he wouldn't even admit he'd removed the $15,000.

Her mind wandered off to the things that happened earlier, most of which gave her a headache until she thought of her kids. Maybe she'd give them a call. She didn't have the heart to tell them their dad had left, though. *Besides, the kids are grown up now. They don't even need me anymore.* That reminder made her heart sink. She started reminiscing about when they were little and how adorable they were when they said their first word or took their first step. That reminded her that she had a box of some cute pictures of them and their drawings. Even though it was past midnight, she brought the box down from the closet and started looking through it. It was a simple white box, a rigid rectangular container with a cover.

She took out a picture of her son, Johnny, and smiled at his dark, brown, wavy hair and soft, brown eyes. He must have been about two in the photo. Growing up, he'd hated that picture of himself, but over the years, it became one of his favorites too. He had berry jam smeared all over his face. *He was so cute in those days. Why can't we have a time machine to help us avoid heartaches and let us linger during the extra good times?*

Debbie's eyes filled with tears. *What has happened to my life?* She clutched the old photos of her children. She felt disappointment, anger, and loneliness all at the same time.

I'm all alone. Debbie's heart was throbbing with pain. Looking through the photos and drawings, she noticed a card she hadn't remembered seeing before.

She didn't remember putting it in the box — although the card looked like something an older person would use rather than a child. It was an ordinary-looking card, with flowers and purple lettering.

Curious, she pulled it out of the box, opened the card, and noticed that it was from Judy, wishing her a happy birthday. The card read:

Thank you for being a great friend. You have the power to change the world. Maybe this will help. Sister, Otter, Subaru.

Debbie was puzzled. How in the world did this card get in there? She would have remembered if Judy had given her a letter. Scanning the letter carefully, she frowned as the note was very cryptic. There were also two lines of URLs written out by hand and a string of numbers. It was as if Judy was trying to tell her something she didn't want just anyone other than Debbie to know. Debbie brought the card downstairs.

The welcoming warmth of her living room did little to calm her nerves. Debbie got out her laptop to look up what some of those things might have meant; she knew that Judy was a big fan of word puzzles.

First, she tried to figure out what "sister, otter, Subaru" could have meant. *It doesn't make any sense. Those words don't go together... Unless it's an acronym.* If it was an acronym, then it would say...

"SOS." Debbie gasped out, perplexed by this newfound clue.

Was Judy crying out for help? Was she trying to say something to me? Or am I just making all of this up? But if that's the case, then what is it?"

Debbie typed the first URL into her computer. A page popped up about the nuclear lab. It appeared to be the general website for the lab. *Why would she write this down?* She typed in the second URL. A page popped up with information on opening a Swiss bank account.

Realization hit her as she rushed to examine the card, exhaling with enlightenment. At the same time, she looked at the numbers written at the bottom of the card— *numbers that could be used for a bank account!*

Was she giving me her bank account number in Switzerland? Why?

Debbie desperately wanted to figure out who killed her friend; she believed she owed that much to her. It seemed she had been in trouble, and now she was dead.

"She was trying to tell me she was in trouble," she breathed out shakily, running a hand through her messy, blonde hair. *I didn't get the point. I could've helped her.*

Debbie was no detective, but she needed to do her best to find her friend's killer. Just then, Fluffy walked down the stairs. He appeared to be groggy since he had just been sleeping. He crawled into her lap and closed his eyes. "You'll help me, won't you, Fluffy?" Fluffy's eyes were still firmly shut as he lay motionless. "Yes, I know you will. You're all I've got left."

Herman

The next day, it was time for work again. Working at the winery wasn't tricky, but not that easy either. Every day, Debbie greeted customers, helped them with wine tasting, and described various wines that might suit their tastes.

She was also in charge of conducting wine tours across the vineyard, answering questions, and giving general information about the winery. She usually loved her job, but she was starting to dread work. Her eagerness to solve Judy's murder was beginning to occupy most of her thoughts, even during working hours.

Debbie wasn't in the mood to work her shift. She was spending the day forcing herself to smile. Her friend and coworker, Patty, spent the day talking incessantly. Usually, Debbie enjoyed her friend's dramatic stories and sarcastic humor. But today, Debbie was only interested in figuring out who could have killed Judy. She finally had a moment away from Patty when she saw a woman with large and expressive brown eyes walk into the winery. The woman had somewhat wrinkled skin and aging spots cleverly concealed with makeup. Debbie knew exactly who she was. She was Trish, the town gossip. *Perhaps Trish knows something.* She rushed over to her.

"Hey, it's nice to see you again," Debbie greeted the older woman with a calculated smile as she walked toward her.

"Oh, Debbie. It's nice to see you too," Trish said, smiling in return.

Debbie asked, "Can I help you with anything? Looking for something specific? I can recommend some fine wines if you'd like." The last time she had seen Trish, she had tried to use her to make a sale. This time, she wanted to use her for a completely different reason.

"No, I'm just planning on getting my usual."

"Have you heard about Judy?" Debbie asked. Trish nodded. "Do you... Do you know anything about why she could have been killed? Or who might have wanted to kill her?" Debbie asked, eager to know anything that might help her solve the case.

Trish paused momentarily, appearing to try to recall recent events. "I honestly can't say I know anyone who would have wanted to kill her. But I know some things about her. For example, I know she was having an affair with her boss, Herman Miller."

"*Her supervisor at the lab*?" Debbie raised her eyebrows in surprise, getting increasingly intrigued about Judy's double life.

Trish nodded. "Yes, that's the one."

"Oh, my goodness. Do you think that's why Dan might have disappeared?"

Trish answered, "I'm not entirely sure what happened to Dan or where he was at the time, but I think there's something suspicious about his disappearance. I think Judy was seeing someone. She implied to me that she was, and she was spending a lot of time with Herman."

"That's so interesting. It's weird how you think you know someone but don't," Debbie mused, utterly caught off-guard by the revelation.

"Yes, that's true. You never know what people are hiding," Trish said with a scrunched-up nose. *This changes everything.* Debbie had a very different impression of Judy. Having an illicit affair sounded like an awful rumor instead of a factual truth, but it would explain a lot.

Maybe she had separated from Dan before. Perhaps they were having problems. Maybe that's why Herman was crying at the memorial service. She had more questions than answers now.

She needed to know; she was dying to uncover the truth behind Judy's unfortunate passing. And there was only one way she could do it, although it was risky since she didn't know him very well. She knew who Herman Miller was. She just needed to know where he lived.

"Debbie?"

Debbie blinked, coming back to reality with Trish's questioning gaze.

"Oh. Uh. You were saying?"

Trish pursed her lips. "I was asking why you suddenly asked if I knew something about the murder. Do you have any leads?"

"No," was her immediate reply. "But I'll try to find the culprit and bring Judy the justice she deserves. By the way, do you know where Herman lives?"

***

That night, Debbie drove over to Herman's house, wasting no time as she pulled up to his driveway. As she got out of her car, she saw the faint shadows of towering trees side-by-side in the forest. It was dark out.

Herman's house was surrounded by a fence, with a gate at the end of the driveway. She pushed it open. The iron bars were as cold as ice, making her clench her hands from the discomfort. As she began to walk toward the house, she could feel the unevenness of the old, cobbled path beneath her. The odd dead leaf crunched underneath her steps. One lonely oak tree stood by the house, swaying in the wind, seeming to whisper to the air and its surroundings. The moon shone bright white in the cloudless sky. It was the only source of light for miles beyond the light coming from Herman's house.

An owl fluttered overhead, its silhouette passing over the grass. The air was cold, and with every breath, Debbie drew in, and a misty exhale followed. Looking at the house from the outside, Debbie could see that the house was tall and thin, made from large dark grey stones that had a rough feel as if sandwiched together by crumbling cement.

Debbie soon found herself face-to-face with her first suspect when knocking at the front door. He was a tall man with white hair...

"Debbie?"

"Hi, Herman. It's been a while."

"Yes. I haven't seen you in a long time. What are you doing here?" Bewilderment was evident in his voice as he tilted his head to the side, frowning at her.

"Well, I was just in the neighborhood, and I thought I'd stop by and say hello," she lied.

"You have never just come over to stop by and say hello." *Boy. Herman is blunt.* She knew the man was skeptical about the real reason she was there.

Defeated, she admitted her actual purpose with a robust and unwavering gaze. "Okay, that's true. I have never come over to say hello. I want to talk to you about Judy."

Herman visibly flinched at her name, nodding lightly as he lowered his gaze to the ground. "Oh yes, Judy. That whole situation is unfortunate."

"Yes, it is regrettable. She was a good friend of mine, too." Debbie asked, looking past Herman, who blocked the view almost immediately. *"Can I come in?"*

The woman noticed how Herman hesitated, nibbling his lower lips slightly as if he didn't want her in the house. He should have invited her in. After waiting a few seconds, Herman pushed the door wider, gesturing for Debbie to walk into his place, where she soon began looking around. People in this town knew each other so well that they usually visited each other often or met for lunch or dinner. Then again, Herman was one of the few that didn't mingle with neighbors.

There was no television, just a sofa, two chairs, and a fireplace; the thick smell of charcoal from the once burning fireplace had spread around the room. They both sat down on the chairs, sitting across from one another.

Debbie coughed as the smell reached her. It appeared that Herman's furniture had once been soft and comfy but were now thin and worn away from all the use. Under the chairs lay a rug stained from the charcoal and shredded at the sides.

"Herman, tell me something. I don't want to seem too forward and insensitive, but there is talk all over town about you and Judy having an affair."

That was a fib. Debbie had only just heard that earlier, so she didn't know if the townspeople had already heard of it before her.

"Me and Judy?" Herman asked, nostrils flaring and eyes wide. He seemed surprised that she had been so straightforward that he nearly choked on the words.

"Yes! You two were having an affair, weren't you?"

"An affair?" the man repeated with a snide scoff. "That's not it at all. Judy was happily married to her husband and would never do that."

"So, what's going on then? Why did you spend so much time together?" Debbie pressed while Herman furrowed his eyebrows at her.

"We were ***friends***."

"What made you become friends in the first place? Surely working together wasn't all there was."

With her direct questioning, Herman couldn't help but give in, sighing at her while pinching the bridge of his nose. He said, "Look, I can tell you, but you have to promise not to tell anybody else."

"You have my word."

Debbie waited as he recalled how he became friends with Judy. "You see, I knew Judy at the lab we both worked in. I was her supervisor, as you may have known. But there was another place where I knew Judy. "

"And that place was?"

"Narcotics Anonymous."

That stunned Debbie, who was gaping at him with a dumbfounded expression.

Herman continued, "She was my sponsor. Judy had told me about this dealer named Philip, who was also my dealer. But it was always like that with her. We had a lot of things in common. So, we connected. It made sense that we should be friends, but there was no affair. That's a rumor."

"Do you think Philip had something to do with her death? Is that why you were crying at the funeral?"

"I'm sorry. I can't answer any more of your questions. There are some things I have to take care of. " Herman was clearly evading the question. That must mean that one of those questions hit too close to home.

"That's fine. But can I use the restroom first? It's urgent!" Debbie bluffed. She just said it so she could roam around and look for anything suspicious. Herman eyed her but said nothing as he nodded, pointing in the direction where the restroom was.

Debbie walked down the hallway toward the restroom. The hallway was dull and smelled of dust. There were paintings hung up of what looked like cranky rich people, their eyes following her every move. As she entered the kitchen, she could see the moonlight shining through the windows, reflecting on the wall opposite her.

Mugs and plates lay on the surface, cold and stained by tea. The sink and taps were made from brass, eroded, and layered in the dirt, still leaking water into the sink. Every time a drop of water fell, an echo passed around the house as though cymbals were being smashed together.

She moved on to the dining room – a large oak table and six matching chairs filled the room. The table had been laid, and the plates and silverware lay there untouched and unused like a forgotten date. Above the table hung a beautiful chandelier twinkling in the moonlight.

The stairs to the second floor were not ordinary stairs — they looked like stairs that would lead to an underground bunker. Debbie wondered what was on the second floor but thought it would be too risky to go find out. She walked along the hallway, noticing a door ajar from one of the many rooms in the house. Intrigued, she quietly slipped through the slightly opened the door to marvel at what was in it.

It was very different from the rest of the house, decorated as if a woman had lived there. It looked like a knitting room since new balls of yarn and thread piled on the boxy hanging shelves. There were large stuffed animals on the bed. There was also a picture album on the wooden table. She picked it up and started looking through it. A lot of the pictures in the book had been torn in half. *I wonder if Herman has a wife or if he has ever been married? Tearing a photo in half? Isn't that something people do after a breakup?*

She left that room, feeling like there were no more clues. She continued down the hall, saw another door ajar, and went in.

Herman is much weirder than I thought he was. This room looked more like a very disorganized, messy office. Debbie saw a phone sitting on the desk. *Maybe that's Herman's cell phone.*

Debbie remembered that he had said something about a man named Philip. As she picked up the phone, she discovered that Herman didn't have a security lock. *That's lucky!* She quickly scrolled through his phone's contact list to find the name.

A Philip was listed. She quickly put the number into her contacts so she could call him later. She put the phone back exactly as she found it.

She couldn't explain it, but Debbie felt a distinct shudder as she looked closer. She looked around and saw things on the walls; many clippings of newspapers were taped to them, with red circles around different parts of different words. Yarn ran from one wall to another, connected and held firmly by push pins.

She started looking around some more, and she noticed there was a theme. Herman circled things like nuclear war, World War three, North Korea, and China in these newspaper clippings. *These articles are clearly about nuclear weapons.*

There were also articles about lasers and chemical warfare. There was one about Herman himself, saying that he had won an award for an experiment that he had done on lasers. She continued looking.

"Interesting. I didn't know Herman was into these things," Debbie mumbled.

"That's because no one has ever dared to enter this room."

She turned around to realize that Herman was standing in the room with her, wordlessly observing her scan the room.

"What are you doing here?" he asked, his voice terrifyingly cold and distant.

"N-nothing. I'm not doing anything," Debbie stuttered, fearing for her life. "I'm sorry. I was just looking for the bathroom, but I got lost."

"The bathroom is down the hall like I told you earlier," Herman pointed out, to which she tried to laugh off awkwardly.

"Y-yeah. You know, I'm not good with directions, so Ha-ha. I saw nothing, and I'm going home now so you can rest. Thank you for having me. Bye!" Debbie almost cried out, hastily making her way out of the house before the man could do something terrible to her.

That was dangerous. I should try to be more careful in the future. Debbie drove away, her hands trembling slightly as she remembered how he looked at her with wild eyes.

Debbie had often thought him odd but never realized he was a lunatic until today.

***

It would've been perfect to have her kids there and their usual routine. But this reality was so bitter that even the tub of ice cream on her dining room table couldn't help her eliminate the feeling of emptiness Debbie had.

Fluffy was staring at her intently, not moving his eyes away from her gaze. "I know you want this. But it's not good for you. You'll get fat. As a matter of fact, it's not good for me either." She brought it into the kitchen and threw it away. *I'm not buying this anymore.*

She headed to bed with a heavy heart, laughing hollowly at the irony of being back at square one.

"What should I do next?" she muttered with closed eyes as she lay on her bed, listing the options she had in mind. She could go hiking. The hiking trail was close, and she could use some exercise to strengthen her core. She could also grocery shop to fill the refrigerator with fresh vegetables and new milk. Her milk was starting to smell funny.

Or you can go and recheck the cabin and see if you can find anything worthwhile. Something inside Debbie whispered, urging her to open her eyes.

It would be a long drive from her house. The roads were narrow, making it hard to see in the dark. *I'll be fine. I'm a klutz, but I'm not an idiot.*

After some deliberation, she decided to go to the cabin. She wasn't entirely sure what she would find; the police had probably taken all the evidence anyway, and nothing would be left. She didn't care. She made the long trip to the cabin, almost driving off the roads a few times because the visibility was so terrible.

She shook her head to clear her mind before getting out of her car and moving to the door. Surprised and a little perturbed, Debbie went to grab the door, only to discover that the lock was still broken, making it very easy to get in.

"Why wouldn't the police fix this?" Thieves could effortlessly get in and never get caught. "How careless," she mumbled quietly as she slowly opened the door, cringing at the creaking sound it made. She stopped halfway, squeezing herself in between the gaps, and tip-toed her way in.

The cabin looked like any other cabin. It was cozy, warm, and away from civilization and polluted air. It was a great place to go to get away from the city.

Debbie was starting to get scared. She didn't know what she was thinking, going there alone with nothing but her fists to protect her. *Yeah, right, like these two fists could save you.* If someone attacked her, Debbie knew she wouldn't stand a chance. She scanned the room for something a bit more damage-dealing. Let's see…a broom, firepit poker, and lamp that looked like mushrooms?

"Yeah, I'd rather go with the poker." She was getting freaked out, so she swiftly picked up the poker and twirled it around as if she were in a James Bond movie.

"Still as clumsy as ever, Debbie."

She flinched, spinning around only to gasp loudly. A man stood in front of her.

"What are you doing here, Ed?" she asked, pointing the firepit poker at him with an accusing glare. "Did you follow me here? Are you stalking me?"

"Calm down. I'm not stalking you," the man said, void of emotion. "I'm just aware of where you are at all times."

Debbie glared at Ed, disturbed by his choice of words. "Isn't that the same as stalking? Why would you even do that? I gave you the chance to choose, move out, or tell me the truth, and you chose to move out."

Being emotional was something she hated. She was so used to being the peppy optimist in the group. Suddenly, she didn't know how to act in this situation, especially when confronted with the man she vowed to stay with in sickness and health.

"This is a lot more complicated than you could imagine," Ed stressed, moving the poker away from him with a soft hand sway. "Debbie, you shouldn't be investigating this murder. It isn't safe."

"How do you know that?"

He paused, visibly pained to even be talking about it. "I can't tell you how I know."

She didn't know why, but something inside her surged like an erupting volcano, spilling frustration and anger like falling debris and burning lava. She glared at him, shaking her fists and flaring her nostrils as she spat.

"That's the problem with you! Your dishonesty! You never tell me anything! You never tell me what's bothering you. That's the problem with all of this. That's the problem with us. And then what? You start following me around. Why would you do something like that? Your behavior is completely unbelievable."

"You don't understand how complicated this whole thing is."

"I **do** understand. I understand it perfectly. I understand that my husband is lying to me. That's all I need to know unless you're willing to tell me the truth. But you won't, will you? Were you even honest with me throughout our marriage?" Debbie asked, visibly hurt and disappointed as her lips quivered and her eyes watered. She got her answer in the form of his hesitation.

"I can't live like this, Ed. I can't live with lies," she whispered, her voice changing from loud and angry to weak and heartbroken as she walked past her husband. Debbie was about to reach the door when Ed held her wrist, stopping her from leaving.

She turned to look at him in confusion and said, "Let go of me, Ed. We're through. I'm leaving."

Ed sighed, rubbing his face crazily, clearly aggravated, using his free hand before staring directly at her with pleading eyes. Never had Debbie seen her husband look so desperate.

Ed said, "I can't tell you anything, Debbie. I wish I could. God, I wish I could tell you. I never wanted to lie, not to you. Not when I vowed to be true."

"Then why did you?" she asked with pain in her voice, searching his eyes for answers. "Why do you continue to lie to me?!"

"Because it isn't safe."

"What do you mean it isn't safe?"

Ed squeezed her wrist quickly, not as tight as before. The man swiftly pulled her into his arms, catching her off guard with a squeak of surprise.

"What are you-?"

"Lower your voice." She was abruptly cut off. "Just promise me to never talk about it to anyone else. Don't ever tell a soul what you know or what you see. Just stay far away from the case."

"Don't talk about it?" she whispered, utterly confused. "Why?"

"Because they may be listening," Ed said, pulling away while giving her arms a firm squeeze. "Please, stop doing whatever you're doing, Debbie. It's too dangerous."

Ed left in his car soon after, leaving a very disoriented Debbie at the cabin alone. She drove home, more confused than ever. Now she could add feeling sad, despondent, discouraged, and frightened to lonely and heartbroken.

What could be going on? How could Ed be involved in this mess? How much does he know that he wouldn't tell me?

Debbie was bewildered. How could she have been married for 25 years and suddenly realize that she couldn't trust her husband? Did she even know the man she had married? She wished that he would just tell her the truth.

Ice Cream

Returning from the cabin made it more apparent to her that there was more than just a murder — more than just Judy being in the wrong place at the wrong time.

Debbie knew she had to get to the bottom of what was going on for her own waning sanity. She paced through the living room, biting her nails in deep concentration on how to gather more information than what she had. That's when she remembered the number she had saved in her contacts.

Debbie searched for her phone. The only way that she could get more information was to contact Phillip at the number she had saved there. Still, it was frightening to think of contacting him after all. She was hesitant, thumb hovering over the displayed contact. Just one tap, and she'd be a step closer to something related to the case that had been haunting her.

He was a drug dealer, of course. But, on the other hand, he was selling narcotics. That wasn't the same as street drugs. Maybe he was safer, more... civil. She honestly had no idea what to expect, but at the same time, she thought she should assume the worst.

Debbie couldn't help but wonder what he was going to be like. *Will he be like the drug dealers in the movies? Covered in tattoos, piercings, red eyes, and unkempt style?*

She had to do something. She impulsively tapped the call button, hearing the ringing sound as she placed it next to her ear. Debbie could feel the loud thumping of her heart through her ears, almost blocking the ringing sound completely. Then the ringing stopped, followed by a skip of her heartbeat and, finally, a man's baritone voice.

"Who is this?" the man called out, his voice sounding indifferent. Debbie forgot what she wanted to say. "Hello? If this is a prank call, I'm hanging up," the man continued.

"Wait!" Debbie immediately spoke, afraid that the man might hang up. "Wait, this isn't a prank call."

"Then? Who is it?" he asked, clearly getting impatient.

"My name... is Debbie."

"Debbie, huh? What do you want, and how did you get this number?"

That was her cue. She swallowed the nervousness that was building in her throat before answering. "I heard about you from my friend, Herman. You know him, right, Philip?"

There was a brief silence.

"Ah, yes. Yes, I know Philip. Why do you ask?"

That sounded a little off, but Debbie chose to shrug it away. She continued, "I see. So, I heard you were the person to go to for..."

"For what?"

"Uh, I was- I am just wondering if I could meet with you to talk about... you know, *narcotics*." She finished, still a little unsure if she sounded like someone who would be looking for narcotics. Still, she decided to pretend that she was interested.

"Hmm, I understand. Yes, that would be fine. We could meet."

Yes! The plan worked. Debbie suppressed the excitement in her tone as she replied, "Okay, great. Can we meet at your house?" She wanted to poke around the place and see if there was something that could give her a clue like she had done at Herman's house.

"No," was his immediate response. "I never meet at my house. I always meet clients somewhere else."

Damn. That would've been too good. "Okay, where would you want to meet?" Debbie questioned, still a bit apprehensive about meeting this stranger.

"We can meet at the Le Petit Ice Cream shop near the town's plaza tomorrow. At noon."

"Okay, that's fine. Ice cream. Yes, let's meet there." She was about to hang up when the man asked another question.

"What made you interested in narcotics, if you don't mind me asking?"

Crap! Debbie hadn't thought this far. What could she say that wouldn't sound like she was lying? What would a person who's interested in narcotics say?

"I'm very interested in narcotics since I've been dealing with a lot of stress lately and just want to… *focus*. Herman said you're the best in town."

"Okay, I understand your interests. I'm flattered to know that I'm being considered the best. And I would love to meet you to talk about it more."

"Great. Tomorrow then."

Debbie couldn't believe she was doing this. Was she going to meet a known drug dealer at an ice cream shop? She must be going crazy to do this voluntarily. But she felt compelled at this point. It was disturbing to know that Judy was murdered and that her murder remained unsolved. To fan the flame further, Ed's behavior was utterly bizarre. She was especially bothered by his comment, *"they might be listening."*

She was eager to understand what this cryptic case was all about. She was smack in the middle of it, whether she wanted to be or not. She was dying to know who had killed her friend, and she needed to understand what had happened. *Judy didn't deserve to die like that.*

***

The next day at noon, Debbie went to meet Philip at the ice cream shop, Le Petit Ice Cream. *Ice cream is a guilty pleasure for a reason. It helps brighten any day, whether a stressful day at work, a summer day spent doing yard work, or after a bad breakup.*

She sat near the entrance by the windows to keep a look out for Philip. Since she was sitting idly and not ordering anything, one clerk eyed her with suspicion and frustration. Debbie could feel the intense stare as she hoped that she could figure out which one of the men walking by was Philip.

I should've ordered something. Debbie reprimanded herself, trying to make herself invisible. A man came over to her, knocking on the table, making Debbie flinch. She snapped her head up, noting how he looked in his 40s. Surprisingly, he was nowhere near what she had imagined.

His hair was grayish but styled into a swept-back look. His beard was well-trimmed, and his features were decent. He was a man who looked like he had his life well-planned. He looked more sophisticated than Herman, whose white hair was uncombed and beard unshaved to complement his absurd style.

"Debbie, correct?" he asked. She recognized his baritone voice.

"Yes, that's me." she faltered, blinking before furrowing her eyebrows. "How did you know?"

"Well, you were sitting here by yourself, looking around like you were waiting for someone, but you weren't sure what he looked like."

"Wow, you're good," Debbie admitted with a nod as he chuckled lowly, which sent shivers running down her spine.

"Indeed, I'm good. What have I gotten myself into? My work requires me to have keen eyes after all."

"Can I buy you some ice cream?" the man asked.

"Huh?"

He pointed at the front of the ice cream shop. "You haven't ordered yet, so I was wondering if you'd like something."

"Oh-uh-okay, sure, yeah." This was interesting. Nothing about this meeting was going as she'd expected. He was offering her ice cream. Debbie wasn't planning on ordering anything. She was planning to cut to the chase, but this man seemed to have another plan. *Is this a date? So, what do I owe him if he buys me ice cream?*

She had reached a new low. They went to the counter in silence, and she started looking at the different flavors on the menu. *So many toppings.* There were so many that it was hard to decide. Should she just get vanilla or chocolate? She thought she should just get something simple and be done with it. But they had all these other things too that also looked good. *Gummy worms. Chocolate chip cookie crumbs. Wow, such delicious toppings.*

"Ready to order?" The clerk who was looking at her earlier spoke with a forced smile. Debbie knew he must've felt annoyed by her staying for half an hour without ordering. She asked for a vanilla chocolate swirl with gummy bears and chocolate chips to make up for it. The clerk smiled a little more, seeming satisfied that Debbie had finally ordered something. "I'll get the same," Phillip said while taking out a card. After they got their ice cream, Phillip turned to face Debbie. "Now, let's get out of here."

"What do you mean get out of here? I thought you wanted to meet here?" she asked with a puzzled look.

Philip said, "Yes, I do. But I don't want to talk here. Let's talk while we walk."

"I see. Okay, I understand." They went outside the ice cream shop and walked together along the sidewalk. The town was relatively small, enshrouded by towering trees and mountain views. Most establishments lined up together on either side of the road. It was a dainty, pretty town where everyone knew everyone.

"So, you expressed on the phone that you had an interest in *narcotics*?" Philip asked, meeting her eyes with a glance as they walked forward. As he said narcotics, he had put his pointer and middle finger up and crunched them down as if he was physically quoting the word *"narcotics"* for whatever reason.

Why is he doing that? Is he not selling narcotics? Does that mean anything? Is this the exact thing that played out before Judy's death?

"I wasn't interested at first, but...." She faltered, gathering her strength to remain stoic and neutral despite her stomach churning in fear. *Here goes nothing.*

"A friend of mine and Herman's was once your client... **Judy**."

She tried to gauge his expression on whether he would break or show any sign of defense, but none appeared. Nothing but a nod after his seemingly periodical silence.

"Yes, I knew Judy."

"And you know about her murder, I assume?" Now, she was pushing her luck. The man gave her another glance, a little longer than a few seconds, before nodding.

"It's regrettable, the thing that happened to her," he said.

The thing? It was a murder? Somehow, his voice sounded so indifferent and heartless to her.

"Yes, it's so sad... I was shocked to hear about her passing. She never did strike me as someone who would have enemies. Who would murder her, right? That's what I thought until Herman revealed that she was into narcotics one day. That's also the time he told me about you." That was only half true, but as close to the truth that she would give him. Philip stopped walking as Debbie did.

"What exactly are you insinuating? That *I* killed her?" he asked, nostrils flaring.

Debbie braced herself, realizing it was too late to chicken out. "No, I'm not insinuating that you killed her. I'm just asking because I want to know what happened to my friend. Where were you that night?"

The woman caught sight of how his fist clenched around the handle of his briefcase; she must've hit a nerve.

"Look, I have a good alibi for that night. Okay?" he started before proceeding to give her a taunting smirk. "And I wouldn't pursue this line of action if I were you. I have people who could mess you up."

What in the world am I doing? Debbie had cold feet, so frightened that her knees almost turned to jelly as she wobbled a little. Her ice cream went flying straight onto his spotless suit.

"O-oh. He had just threatened her, and now she was, spilling ice cream on him. Oh my God- I'm sorry. Let me just-" she stammered, impulsively scooping the spilled cold dessert from his suit using her bare hands.

Great job. Debbie. Now he'll have more reasons to consider putting you on his hit list. She gulped, shaky pupils darting up to see his face. *Will he kill me out of anger now that I've spilled on him? Lord, have mercy, I still have so much to-*

"It's fine. You didn't have to scoop the ice cream with your hands," he said as he pulled out a clean handkerchief to wipe the dirtied spot. Debbie stepped away, hands now sticky with ice cream as she looked at him, dumbfounded.

"Listen, I'll cut to the chase since it looks like you lied about why you wanted to meet me. Did Judy give you the papers?" Philip asked, eyes now a little darker and menacing.

Papers? What papers? Isn't he supposed to be a drug dealer?

"Look," he added when Debbie failed to reply, "if I get the papers, this will all go away. Everything will go away. Your husband will be free of his obligations."

... Ed's obligations?

"What obligations? What does my husband have to do with this? How do you know my husband?"

Debbie flinched away when he took a step forward. She took two steps backward, trembling terribly.

"Don't take too long," he said, eyes shifting to look past her for a moment before backing away. "As I said before, I have people who could mess you up," he threatened again before disappearing into the crowd.

Debbie remained standing there, shivering with terror.

***

As Debbie sat in the kitchen of her suburban home, she regretted her decision to start investigating Judy's murder. She wondered what she should do about it. She had promised Herman that she wouldn't say anything about his narcotics problem, but maybe it was time to get the police involved. Just then, Fluffy jumped on her lap.

"I don't have to keep my word to a man who may be a murderer, right? What do you think, Fluffy?" The dog barked. She sighed in frustration. "I can't hide something from the police," she continued. Debbie had met the handsome 40-year-old detective, Matthew, shortly after she had found Judy's body. She had felt at ease with him right away, despite the harrowing situation at the cabin.

"Matthew is a good man," she said to Fluffy. "He's very good-natured and trustworthy. I should tell him everything I know. Also, he's hot!"

As if on cue, the doorbell rang. Debbie answered the door, and detective Matthew stood there, looking more handsome than ever with his charming smile. *Great timing.*

The two of them sat down as she told Matthew everything about what had been going on over some hot cocoa. She told him about her husband's comments when he said that "they might be listening" and that his behavior had changed. She also told him about Herman and their conversation, as well as her conversation with Philip.

She told Matthew how Philip had threatened her and said *"narcotics"* while physically quoting it with his hands, which made no sense to her. Matthew replied, "It would be beneficial for us and for you to find those papers as quickly as possible."

Debbie froze midway from sipping her cocoa. *How does Matthew know about these papers?* She did mention her conversation with Philip but nothing about "the papers." She didn't even know what they were. And Judy had never given her anything to her knowledge.

"I'm sorry. But I'm not following what you're saying. Judy never gave me anything."

"Okay, at least look around and see if you can figure it out. Judy may have given it to you in a way that you don't realize yet. I'm sure it's somewhere. She likely gave them to you, and you don't realize exactly yet."

Matthew also told her that he believed Herman was having an affair with Judy, according to the evidence he collected. He added that the woman that had been ripped out of those pictures in Herman's house was likely Judy.

Let's Visit

The next day, Debbie went back to the winery. Upon arriving, she had been appointed to greet the customers at the front door. The day seemed endless. She caught herself thinking about Herman and Judy's affair the whole day. She desperately wanted to go to his house and talk to him again, hoping that he would say something implicating and admit to the affair.

When work finally ended, Debbie rushed to her car. Patty came out and started talking to her. She didn't want to be rude since her friend simply asked if she had been feeling better, concerned about Debbie's separation from her husband. However, as much as she appreciated her concern, time wasn't waiting for anyone, most certainly not for her. Philip's threat was engraved in her mind.

"I'm sorry, Patty, but I have to go," she said, fumbling with her keys.

"Where are you headed to that you're in such a rush?" Patty asked, cocking her head to the side in confusion.

"I'm headed to Herman's house." Debbie decided to be transparent. Patty deserved that much. Her transparency only caused her more problems.

"Why would you want to go to his house? He's a dangerous man! You shouldn't have anything to do with him. He could hurt you!" Patty exclaimed, gazing worriedly at her seemingly reckless friend, who had finally found her car keys. *Why do I have so many keys? Only God knows...*

"No, I don't think so... I don't think he would hurt me."

"And what's your proof?" Patty raised an eyebrow, clearly not buying her words.

"I've talked to him once. I think he thinks of me as a friend and, sure, he seems a little crazy, but why would he hurt me? I don't think he would if I don't give him a reason to," Debbie answered, opening her car door only for Patty to slam it shut, fuming with a deeper frown.

"Well, I don't feel comfortable about you going alone. I'm coming, and I won't let you drive off until you promise me I can follow you there."

"No, Patty. You don't have to do that. I'll be fine."

"I'm not convinced."

Debbie sighed, rubbing her temples. "Honestly, I'll be okay. Stop worrying so much!"

"I don't feel comfortable with this at all, and you can't tell me not to worry when you're impulsively doing things that could get you literally killed! So, you either let me go with you, or I won't let you go there."

Good God, Patty sure can be persistent when she wants to be. With a defeated grunt, Debbie said, "Okay, fine, you can come. But you won't be saying anything and doing anything suspicious. Got it?"

Patty grinned. "Pinky, promise!" She put out her pinky.

They drove together towards Herman's house in separate cars. Debbie hadn't realized how unnatural it would be to just show up at his door again, but it was even worse with Patty next to her this time. She couldn't think of any excuse why Patty would be with her or a reason why she had just suddenly shown up at his house once more.

Debbie nearly had a heart attack when Patty ran towards the door, acting like she was about to loudly knock. Debbie yanked her back with a reprimanding scowl.

"I thought I told you not to do anything stupid?!" she hissed, but Patty avoided her gaze with an awkward and hushed laugh.

"Yeah, I was just going to knock for us both."

"You weren't just going to knock. You looked like you wanted to bang your fist on the door," Debbie stated in exasperation, demanding that Patty not barge as she softly knocked on the door and rang the doorbell.

Weird. Herman opened it for me the first time I rang the doorbell.

"Maybe he's sleeping? Or wearing headphones?" Patty asked.

"Does Herman look like the type of man who would wear headphones to you?" Debbie deadpanned before trying to ring the doorbell again. There was still no answer.

It was getting a lot stranger as she looked around. Everything was still in place; his lawn looked shabby with wacky stone gnomes and unevenly cut grass. Debbie couldn't figure out how Herman could be so unbothered as to not repair his porch when he had more than enough money. She supposed the man had other things to focus on that required more attention than his own house.

"Debbie, look." Patty was pointing at the lock that appeared to be broken. It looked broken the same way the cabin's safety had been, almost terrifyingly identical.

She had two options: enter the house without thinking or be more rational and call Matthew to investigate. Debbie chose the first option.

"You stay here in case something bad happens. If I don't return in 5 minutes, call the cops," she told Patty with a rugged look. Patty's facial expression implied that she did not like this plan.

"But-"

"Please, Patty. We can't have both of us be put in danger. Someone has to call the cops if this goes downhill."

"Fine. But be careful, and don't hesitate to bolt out of the house if you see anything remotely dangerous."

Debbie nodded and smiled at her friend before carefully opening the door and walking in, feeling every hair of her body standing up.

Why is his lock broken? Where is he? Who could have done it? She nearly tripped over an open book that was lying on the floor. She walked through the hallway toward his living room.

I hope Herman doesn't shoot me, mistaking me for an intruder.

"Herman," she called out to him. "It's me, Debbie. I'm just wondering if you are okay. I saw your broken lock, so I got worried."

There was no answer.

"Herman? Are you there? Can you make any noise?" She gulped, sweating in fright as her breathing gradually became labored.

She entered his living room and froze, almost retching at the first sight that greeted her eyes.

There, in the middle of the room, was a body.

Herman Miller was dead.

Did you enjoy this book?

If so, please leave a review on Amazon!

https://www.amazon.com/review/create-review/?ie=UTF8&channel=glance-detail&asin=B0B5SF6FN6

Ready for more? Follow this and other favorites below!

https://www.ttpublishinghouse.com/legendsreborn

https://www.ttpublishinghouse.com/7wishes

https://www.ttpublishinghouse.com/mallcadet

www.ingramcontent.com/pod-product-compliance
Lightning Source LLC
Chambersburg PA
CBHW051937150726
47999CB00006B/2260